Lucy Ela Walmsley loves to write magical stories! Her goal is to inspire children's imaginations and let them grow endlessly. The world is a beautiful place. Get lost in a crazy, magical, adventurous book whilst lying in the bluebells on a summer day. Read as much as you can to your children and let their imaginations grow into something wonderful!

Keeping our environment and this world we live in clean and alive is very important. Nature plays such an important part and the bees are now unfortunately endangered. Bees play a huge part in our environment and it would have a catastrophic impact on us and our environment if we lost them. There are many things that we are able to do to help. If you would like more information, please visit www.friendsoftheearth.uk

D1514134

For my grandad (Dede) Ahmet C Gazioglu

4th February 1931- 4th September 2020

An inspirational writer and author of many bestselling books worldwide. A journalist, researcher, teacher and headmaster, advisor and then special advisor to the founding president of the Turkish Republic of North Cyprus, and also the first ever UK Representative of the Turkish Cypriot people.

You fought for what you believed in and you helped many.

The Faery Tales
The Crowning of Queen Bee.

Lucy Ela Walmsley
Illustrated By: Ellie Usher

AUSTIN MACAULEY PUBLISHERS™
LONDON • CAMBRIDGE • NEW YORK • SHARJAH

A CIP catalogue record for this title is available from the British Library.

ISBN 9781398438002 (Paperback)
ISBN 9781398438019 (ePub e-book)

www.austinmacauley.com

First Published (2021)
Austin Macauley Publishers Ltd
25 Canada Square
Canary Wharf
London
E14 5LQ

I would like to say thank you to my mum, who always believed. A rose always grows through the thorns creating goodness for all around it.

You fought for what you believed in and you helped many.

Once Upon a Faery Tale the faeries were getting ready
for a big day.
For today was the crowning of Queen Bee!

The bumble bees, Buzz and Honey, were waiting excitedly outside the faeries' bedroom window. This special occasion didn't happen very often. So today was a very special day.

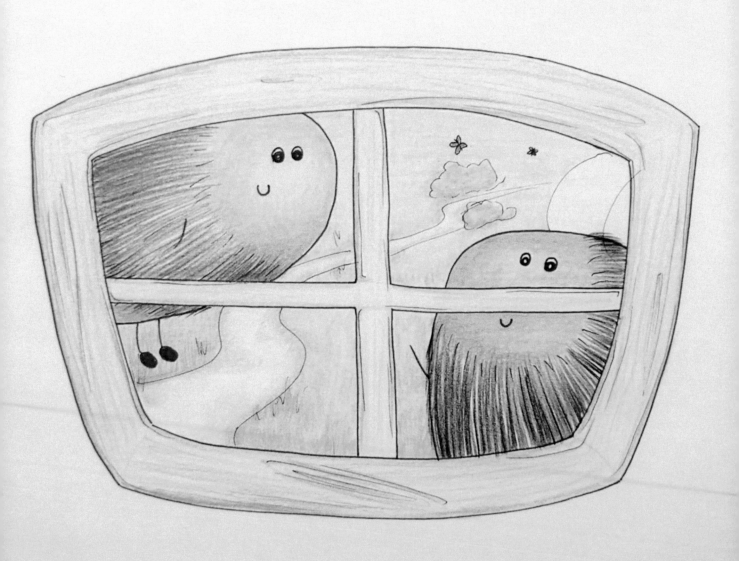

"Right faeries, are we all ready?" Ember asked.
"We certainly are!" the other three faeries replied with
excitement in their voices.
Buzz and Honey, the bumble bees, buzzed away
happily wiggling their bottoms.

The faeries jumped on Buzz and Honey's fluffy bumble
bee backs and flew off to the big ceremony.
Willow and Delta were on Buzz and Aria and Ember
went on Honey.
They flew all through Glenn Acre and deep into The
Enchanted Woods until they could hear The Singing
Frogs and The June Bugs Band. The beautiful sounds
of their music bounced through the trees and all
around the forest.

Delta jumped off from Buzz and went to take her
seat next to Caspian, her brother, and her mother
and father. The other faeries found their families too
and took their seats, ready and waiting for the big
ceremony to begin.

Suddenly it all went very quiet.
"SHHHHHHHHHH, SHHHHHHHHHH" Mr Cricket hopped
up onto the stage.
"My fellow bees, faeries and gentle bugs, may you now
please be seated" he announced.
The faeries all sat down on their seats and the Singing
Frogs and the June Bugs Band started up. The June
Bugs were playing their bluebell trumpets and the
frogs were singing the anthem of the forest.

Then everyone made way. For there was a rather eye catching golden coloured bee flying smoothly through the parted crowds. It was Queen Bee. And today was her Crowning Day. She would be officially the Queen Bee of Glenn Acre.

Buzz and Honey bowed their heads down as the gracious, soon to be, Queen Bee flew past them.

Everyone took their seats. Mr Cricket then spoke. "Faeries and gentle bugs. As you know, today we officially have a new Queen Bee. And the time has come for our queen to be crowned".

There was a great cheer.

"This is so exciting!" Delta whispered to her brother Caspian.

"Doesn't she look pretty?" Willow whispered to Ember who was sitting in front of her. Ember nodded her head.

Mr Cricket then began the ceremony. Queen Bee
happily buzzed away.
"I now crown you Queen Bee. Queen Bee of Glenn
Acre and all of The Faerylands" said Mr Cricket.
He turned to get the crown from behind him.
"Oh no! The crown is gone! Someone's stolen it!"
he shouted.
Everyone gasped in horror.

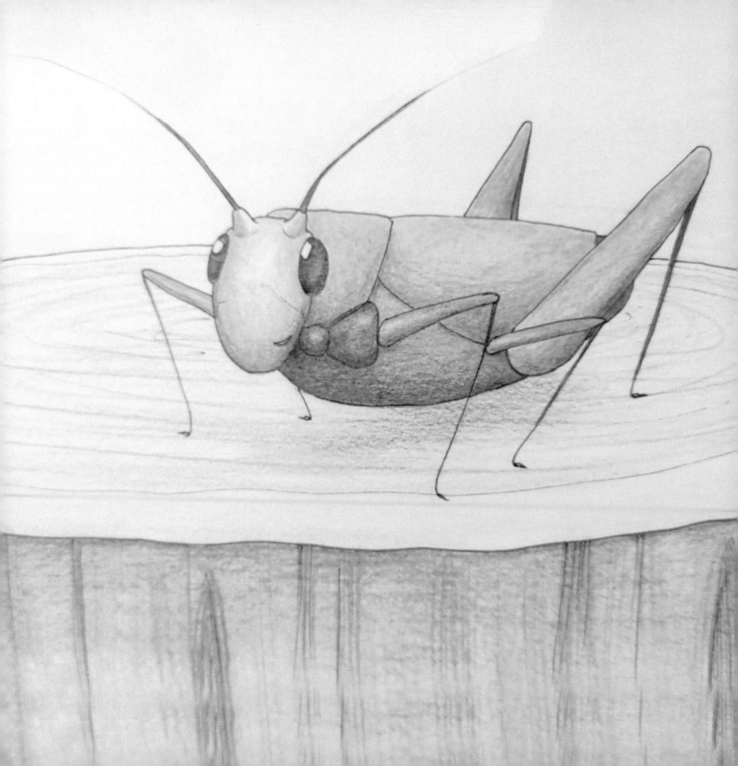

Queen Bee suddenly stopped her happy buzzing. Mr Cricket was frantically looking around for it.
The crowd gasped.
"Oh no" Delta whispered to her brother Caspian.
All the faeries and gentle bugs in the crowd started to search around for the crown.
"We have to help find it " Delta said to Caspian as the other faery friends flew over to them.
So Caspian, Delta, Willow, Ember and Aria started searching around for the crown.

After a while of the crowd all searching frantically
for Queen Bees crown, Aria spotted Dawn and Luna
peeking from behind a tall oak tree.
She flew over to them followed by the other faeries.
Dawn and Luna both looked awkwardly at the four
faery best friends.
Luna was hiding something behind her, and Dawn was
looking sheepishly at the floor.

"We didn't realise that this was THE crown when we took it" Dawn said looking up.

"We just found it sitting there on the table on the side and decided that while no one was around, that we could play a game. We were pretending to be the Princess Faeries" Luna said bringing her hands out from behind her back clutching the crown.

"We got carried away playing with it and then went to put it back but the ceremony had begun" Dawn said. Ember and Willow looked at each other.

Both Luna and Dawn looked at each other.

"And then we hid behind this big oak tree because we thought everyone would be so angry with us and think that we'd stolen it!" explained Luna.

Dawn looked down again at the floor rather ashamed.

"Have we ruined the ceremony?" she said.

Aria went over to Dawn "No, not if you give it back and apologise" she told Dawn.

All of the faeries flittered back towards the crowds.
Where everyone was still searching around for the
crown. Luna was holding the crown with Dawn next to
her as they flew in front.
Delta, Aria, Ember and Willow followed behind.

Mr Cricket spotted them coming and saw that Luna holding the crown.

"You found it!" he happily shouted.

Everyone stopped and looked at the faeries.

"Well no, actually we had it the whole time" Luna confessed to Mr Cricket.

"So, you stole it?!" Mr Cricket asked sounding rather shocked.

"No, we didn't steal it, we didn't know it was THE crown. We saw it sitting there and thought it would be fun to borrow it and play a game. And then the ceremony began, and we realised what was going on, we thought everyone would be upset and think that we had stolen it." Luna tried to explain.

"And we were scared" said Dawn

Willow stepped forward and prompted Luna and Dawn
"It was a mistake and they realised and bought it back".
"We didn't mean to cause such a commotion and we are very,
very sorry" Dawn told Mr Cricket.
The crowd then parted and made way. Then Queen Bee came
flying through to the faeries.
All of the faeries curtsied and bowed their heads for
Queen Bee.

Queen Bee buzzed to Mr Cricket to lean in so she could speak to him.
"Okay, Okay, AHHHH I SEE" Mr Cricket responded to Queen Bee.
The crowd started whispering in confusion.

"Queen Bee would like to thank you for bringing her crown back. She understands it was a misunderstanding and that you are trying to do the right thing by bringing it back" Mr Cricket told the faeries.

Queen Bee buzzed approvingly.

Mr Cricket hopped back to the stage.

"Faeries and gentle bugs. We have the crown and shall now proceed with the ceremony".

This time Mr Cricket could actually place the crown on Queen Bees head.

All of the faeries and gentle bugs flittered and buzzed back to their seats and watched the ceremony of the crowning of Queen Bee. It was a magnificent ceremony, and everyone was very happy and excited to have a new Queen Bee of the Enchanted Forest.

Being led through the crowds by her ladybird guards, Queen Bee looked at the faeries and gave them a little buzz as a gesture of appreciation.

On the way to the celebration party, Dawn and Luna joined the faeries and their bumble bees, Buzz and Honey. They all danced together to The Singing Frogs and the June Bugs Band with their guest singer, who was in fact Queen Bee. This Queen needed no stage name as she was the greatest singer in The Enchanted Forest.

"Thank you for helping us" Dawn told the four faery best friends.

"We are grateful. And you showed us that facing up to what we did, and apologising was the right thing to do" Luna added.

It was a great celebration!
Everyone in Glenn Acre and The Enchanted Forest
thoroughly enjoyed themselves.
"What a great day it's been" Ember said happily to
her friends.
"It just shows that doing the right thing is always best" Aria
said smiling at Luna and Dawn.
Dawn and Luna's faces lit up into big smiles and they all had
a group hug.
Buzz and Honey buzzed away happily wiggling their fuzzy
bottoms in unison.

THE END.

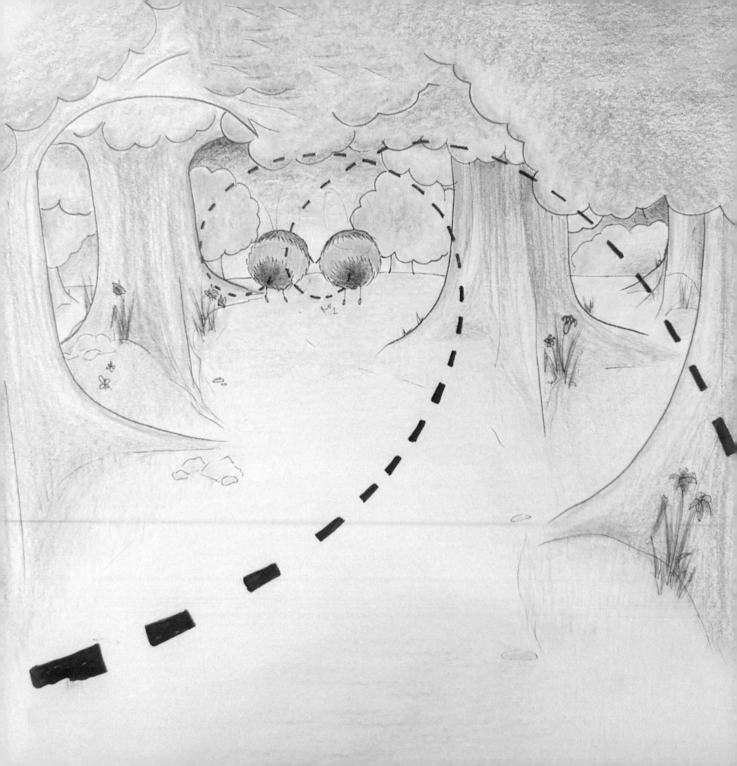